THE THEORY OF RELATIVITY

*A Collection of
Short Stories and Poems*

VAIBHAVI GAIHA

Dallah Books
An Imprint of Gulf Book Services LTD.

Published by: Dallah Books
                An imprint of
                Gulf Book Service Ltd
                20-22 Wenlock Road, London.
                NI 7GU
                UK
                Email: info@gulfbooks.co.uk

ISBN: 978-1-7397687-0-6

Dedicated to the teachers who stood by me no matter what, with formal title and without. You know who you are.

Prologue

The thought of writing this book came to me when I was in 10th standard. I had just moved from the US to India, and it was 2017, the year in which board exams had been made compulsory. In a desperate attempt to understand and process everything that was happening around me- the change in atmosphere, the people, the fear of the board exams, I started to write short memoirs and stories on the bus to school. The morning fresh air, accompanied by delightful lush greenery that I absorbed out of the window encouraged me. This book has been written between lunch breaks and bus stops. Of course, at the time, I was unsure of whether I would actually succeed in creating a book and I didn't know if I wanted the stories to be published either. The pandemic, however, has taught me that life is short and that it isn't worth living if we aren't doing impulsive things now and then. A part of me has always wanted to do something like this for fun. So I don't care much for if the writing isn't perfect or if the book doesn't reach a million people. It is a part of me and always will be.

What I hope for whoever does read this book is that it makes them think about things. About the simple things in life and about how everyone views the world differently. About dreams, and about aspirations- or perhaps a lack thereof. A perspective of reality is what I gained from observing the most boring and simple things in life and writing all these "boring" stories- how everything we know and see is relative to another.

Contents

The House

The house had always been very different. Always another cut. Its walls were not painted white, but instead a steady flow of various designs. Crochet, geometrical, elegant spirals. The windows were very different too. There were four you could see on the outside. One was a huge, plain circle. Another was in the shape of a diamond. The next in the style of a French window, with its diagonal sills and tilted glass. The fourth was a square, it's sills the colour of black tar. It was a very curious window, that one. It was plain, and had no design. It stood there solemnly, as if begging for respect. Its place in the extraordinary house. Trying and failing to compete with the other windows. It was quite small. But it was the clearest of them all. So clear, that if you went to the attic and tried to look through, you would probably hit your nose on the glass, assuming the glass never existed, or did further away.

The roof was the most exquisite of them all. The most different. At least in the neighbourhood. If you ever came to Bombay and observed the buildings, you would see the same thing everywhere. Grey, or white buildings, with rooms full of boundless life. Laughter, and sorrow. Presence, and absence. Peace, and cacophony. Love and war. But if one went to the last row of the buildings starting in Andheri, where the houses ended and the forest started, one would not think of it much. Underestimation is almost inevitable. Almost. Intricate grooves are carved upon the wood, with faces and pictures of nature painted with the most beautiful of natural colours. Once in a while the birds would invite the children to the greenery. Away from their phones. Away from their laptops or video games. Where curious children once played and laughed, now there is serenity. Once in a while the monkeys would swoop down to see if any mangoes were left. Only they knew that they existed there. The bountiful and ever replenishing fruits of the secluded area were known only to animals.

However, even those who had visited the place, had not really seen it. They had not stopped to listen to it. The house unseen and yet visible. The house that not only communicated within itself- chatter between the different rooms and windows, but also sent messages to the trees around it.

When the annual whisper of winter drifted through the air, its wood kept the house warm. And when the summer breeze would come, the concrete kept it cool. The weather the rest of the city faced was much different from what the house endured. For it, the winters were colder, and the summers, hotter. When spring would come, the house would be covered on the outside with flowers and green creepers, and during autumn, perhaps it was the only place in the city you could see the pink and red leaves swaying about, gently falling off before the winter.

The rooms in the house were most peculiar, for they did not seem to be consistent in design. One of them was quite large, and had pale green walls and pretty windows. The sills of the windows were carved to look like laced doily, and the inbuilt cupboards were made of dark rosewood. It seemed perhaps, an old couple would love to stay here, in this very room, reminiscing about the past of their love, and enjoying each other's company for the rest of their lives. Situated in the middle was a bed, an old bed made of wood that also had a tinge of red in it. But it wasn't rose, and nor was it teak. It was, however, functional, and much sturdier than the rest of the furniture in the room and perhaps the house. Behind it, the wall had two holes, indicating some decorative piece had been hung there.

Right next to it was another room, which had its own attached bathroom. Now this room was different. The walls were an off-white colour, rugged looking, but never dirty. The floor was wooden, and parts of it creaked when walked upon. The winters urged the fireplace to awaken every year, and the wood would turn to coal, and the coal to ashes. The bed in the middle, large as it was, was enough to warm whoever would want to sleep in it. Alas, for the house had never been inhabited for long.

These two rooms were at the end of a long corridor, which possessed two more rooms. The doors that these other rooms had were different, and they looked as though they had been made of stone. The heavy black rectangles of stone stood there, as if looking for the strongest of men, or anyone who dared to try to move them. They covered, however, the plainest rooms in the whole house, each with pale colours on the walls and simple beds. There was a lonely nightstand in each room.

However, if you were to go to their bathrooms, you would notice the inner walls first. Laced with the prettiest of shimmering blue and pink tiles, the walls glistened in whatever light the morning seemed to offer. The floor as well, was covered with these tiles. The bathtub was golden, and the mirror right in front of someone would make them feel strangely underdressed for the venue. As plain and simple as the rooms were, their bathrooms exuded luxury and brilliance.

The kitchen was normal. Perhaps the most normal room in the house. Its cupboards were wooden, and had metal handles, the countertop was marble, and the floors were checked. In this painfully simple room, designed by painfully simple people, the most interesting thing was the fact that many seemed to not be able to stand it. A mere hour of being in the kitchen was sure to send someone spiralling down vague and ambiguous feelings of sadness, and thoughts of the purpose of life and the meaning of it all overwhelmed them. It was just one of those rooms, though nothing was wrong with it, that there was this constant feeling of hopelessness and despair that just did not go away. Subtle, yet visible, if one were to visit this house, this room was the most off-putting.

The outside of the house was just as strange and bizarre. Every window was different, but the most prominent part of the house was how the roof jutted out aggressively, threatening to pierce any tree that dared grow in front of it. A part of it had Tibetan engravings and carved deities, another part had polka dots made with black and grey. The many designs of the top of the house stopped as soon as they touched the windows, and after that, the house was plain except for the door. The door was painted in an obnoxious, loud red colour, and had a grey metal doorknob.

The house that sat, at the end of the line of the ordinary houses, often compelled people to wonder what was in it. And if anyone was brave enough to seek out the owner to be granted permission to visit it, they would see the most beautiful rooms, and the few more terrifying ones. The interiors of the house inexplicably drew people in, and everyone who visited it left with the vague feeling they had seen all the people in the world, they had met everyone there was to meet, and they had discovered the beauty as well as the horror of the different consciences of all the people in the world. And yet they did not fully see the house, and neither did they listen to it.

Decisions

Enjoying the soft breeze brushing against her face, she grew silent. The silent and calming hum of the bus's engine seemed to contain the key to one of life's simpler pleasures. The trees around the bus caressed the windows, and many dropped a few burdensome leaves. As the bus drove through slim meandering streets, and stopped to pick up the usual passengers, a squirrel ran across the fence of a bungalow. It was pleasant. The feeling of carefreeness, along the silent hullabaloo of the children in the bus, compelled her to think about school. The sun's light was dimmed by the chill of the morning, and whatever light reached the Earth at seven am, seemed to be reflected mainly by the variety of flowers whizzing past the bus- modest, but noticeable. The buzz of the cars on the road contrasted with the soft, lapping sounds of the lakes they passed. Far off buildings seemed very far off, and life was passing slowly, as if to marvel at the passing thoughts of children.

She proceeded to think about school. She thought about homework and college. Thoughts about the Boards, and what she would do once she got through college came to mind. Suddenly she said to herself – 'Science or Language'. The dilemma she faced throughout her life was now demanding a decision. 'Right now. Right here, in the bus. Choose.' The voice grew louder and louder. Life, which was sitting on the bus looked at her sternly, bored, almost, as if it saw this kind of decision being made every day. 'Both', she'd usually respond, postponing the decision every time. But this time, she knew she didn't have a third option.

Forcefully, the voice proceeded to tell her to be calm. Someday, she was going to make the choice. Why not today? Why not now?

The bus grew cold, and the peace she had been experiencing started to dissipate. The flowers seemed dull, and lifeless. The noise of the bus was ever more noticeable. The girl closed her eyes, trying to ignore her thoughts. But life looked, waiting impatiently. Glancing at time occasionally. It might have just been her imagination, but it looked like the most real thing around her, and the bus suddenly seemed surreal, as if it was only a background, a setting for what truly was real, the decision. The two options hovered before her eyes. Each child seemed to be saying 'Science' or 'Language'; Science or Language. The voices grew louder and louder. Life smirked mockingly. She had passion for both subjects, but she knew she could only choose one for her main career. She glanced at a first aid kit. It seemed to say 'Science or Language' too. She blinked in surprise.

As the voices grew louder, the pressure increased. The tension in the atmosphere crystallized, but the voice pressed on. Trying to divert her attention, she looked through the window. But everywhere, all she could see was life's mocking face looking back at her, its eyes the colour of the future, emboldened with the power to change everything. Her heart beat was increasing steadily. Suddenly, everything stopped. Life disappeared. The scenery stopped moving. Fate had to take over the reins now. Time was up. The bus had arrived.

Results

It was just after English class. An unsettling feeling had come over her before the class, but after it was over, it had started to feel like the shards of a broken mirror were cutting through her stomach. A familiar feeling, it was. But maybe not familiar enough. This feeling wasn't like sadness. It was a different kind of sadness, maybe. However different, this feeling was even more crippling than sadness. The classroom was an embryo for this feeling, a culture for this English class. It was the cold and bitter feeling that silenced the usually loud noise and chatter of the classroom today.

Every time she thought she should be confident; she'd receive a result less than what she'd expected. It felt as if, even the tiniest bit of prediction she wanted to make, she shouldn't, some sort of cruel joke would make it so that she regretted being comfortable with her confidence before. *So last time it was 37 out of 40. Doubling that, I'd get 74 out of 80. Hopefully more. No, definitely more. The exam went so well.* Thoughts like this came often. Usually accompanied by disappointment. But this later fact was obviously untrue. Surely it couldn't happen so many times?

Forty-one faces appeared in front of the classroom. Most were sad, some were happy. Others looked like the colour was drained out of their faces. Each name was called, whispering friends asked about the results, and time ticked by, sound stepped back, unwilling to engage. The last roll number was called, and the girl got up, gulped, and put her hands forward. A heavy stack of papers touched her hand, and she opened her previously closed eyes. There wasn't enough time for a deep breath, because she was too curious. Seventy out of eighty. Anger boiled its way through to the top, and shock also took over. Going through her paper, she noticed the mistakes she had made. English was always a subject that made her happy. How could she possibly lose ten whole points? The feeling of apprehension left, and it was the feeling of helplessness and the fact that all her hopes came crashing down, and her soul cried, only aiding this feeling.

The rest of the class was spent with students hovering around the teacher like bees. 'Half a mark, ma'am,' someone pleaded. Another asked if she could please check the 'story' section again. *This was the only paper I thought I could get a 100 percent on.* It seemed like the midterm results wouldn't end up helping her after all. The huge barrier of uncertainty rose up. She tried to break it this time, but now she knew. She had run headlong towards the large grey wall of the barrier, damaging her head in hopes of breaking it. The only mark she saw on it was a small niche, which seemed like the impression of her head.

Broken

Beaten up and broken down, the void of darkness overcame her. No longer did she feel the saline drops of water running down her cheeks. No longer did she care. Every bare molecule of her existence protested against perseverance. But no longer was she able to suppress the initially tiny voice in herself. To give up was an option, not a choice.

To defy herself was the ultimate battle. A war that waged on forever in her heart, and was neither lost nor won. It simply existed. Existed, and caused turmoil. Turmoil that lasted forever. Turmoil that would never give in, just like that little voice. That tiny voice that summed up all her feelings, and led them to the cliff of consciousness, where she could hear them. But this time, the voice said something different. This time, it did not fade. This time, it persevered, just as it asked to do. It did not simply exist; it calmly ordered. No, it requested. Soft and simple, its message was clear. 'To give up is to accept defeat.' Over, and over, and over again it repeated, forcing the war to be even more violent. And yet, this time, the voice had made an ally. Guilt's soldiers flooded the battlefield. Her vision blurred as she opened her eyes. The calm voice took over. Her hand, defying her wishes, picked up the book, and flipped to chapter three. The steady stream of water was blocked by courage. Finally, the words made sense. The battle had been won.

A Citizen of the World

It was weird. It felt horrible. It was when I couldn't shake the feeling, that somehow somewhere down the road, I'd started feeling like a foreigner in my own country. Two or three years abroad made me feel like my nation is the best, and yet, when I came back, that idealized view shattered when reality hits me. I shouldn't have an identity crisis, but sometimes I do. When everyone treated me like an outsider, when people judged me, based on where I have lived. Because I am Indian by heart, brain and passport, but to others, it's a surprise I can speak Hindi. They laugh when I fail to put my belt in through one loop. I haven't used uniforms in a while now. They feel threatened when I start doing well in class because to them, I'm no longer Indian. 'That new girl, she has green hair! It looks so weird.' This is not what I came for. I came here because this is where I should belong, this is where I should fit in. This is where I thought the monachopsis would stop. This is where I constantly feel that all those days when I refused to sing a foreign national anthem, refused to be associated with another country, were perhaps worthless. No value. Nothing. I was an outsider there; I am an outsider here. I can't tell if the people I do know, the people who I assume are my friends are really the way they are with me the way they are with others. If I could ever truly make friends who are just as close as people are with each other here. They've known each other forever, they've grown up together. You can't possibly imitate that bond. Everyone knows everyone, and I'm not anyone. They shouldn't have to do this all the time, walk on eggshells around me. 'Go away'. I've been doing that for the past few years. Okay then, if not for this, I came for the food, the festivals, the life. At least people speak Hindi here, if not particularly with me. At least I can stand up proudly and sing the national anthem in the morning assembly, I can marvel at their shocked faces, and I can just be a better me. I'm staying, because I owe it to my country, I feel I am worth something, and that worth belongs where I was born. I am the result of the experiences I've had with people around the world, the languages they speak and the diverse cultures I have been exposed to. It makes me grateful to be able to say that I experienced so many cultures and so many different kinds of people. The beauty of it all often overwhelms me, when I think about the lives I've led. And in all this diversity, in all the gloriousness of the differences in people, genetic and otherwise, I feel a sense of belonging and some sense of the togetherness us human beings should have. I belong everywhere and with everyone I have met. I'm staying here, because this is what I am. A citizen of the world, with an Indian passport.

Diwali and Happiness

It was that time of the year again. The girl was happy. There was no school for some time. Days were spent in leisure, with happiness, and she realized it was one of those times that she felt happy to be back home. It was seven pm. Going out of the house, she smelled a heavenly smell. It was as if someone had shot happiness up her nostrils. Inhaling deeply, she closed her eyes. She was in the middle of the rows of houses in the colony. Sigh. It smelled of delicious sweetmeats, and namkeen. The sound of someone nearby frying the shakarpara, combined with this smell, made for a virtual image in her mind that no technology could mimic. The aroma smelt of part sugar, part flour, sizzled in love. Every single house emitted warmth. Fairy lights and decorated gardens were twinkling as if to lure fairies themselves. The soft breeze, although consisting of a southern air, managed to disperse the smell all around. This is my happy place, she thought. She could almost taste the sweets, as she felt as though time had stopped to let this feeling go on and on. Of-course everyone was happy. Of-course everyone was content. The smell was so aromatic, it engulfed everyone, and it seemed to announce to everyone, Diwali was here. Happiness had spread.

A Musical Lunch

She sat down, and ate her lunch. Today, it was paratha, and a kind of candy called 'fruit by the foot'. In blissful reverie and deep thinking, she remembered her previous school. Eventually her thoughts returned to the present, and to her brother, who often visited her in recess. Today, it didn't seem he would. Only fifteen minutes were left till the end of the lunch break. Sighing to herself, she got up, and packed her lunch away. The noise of the classroom was unbearable, and yet made no difference to her. Walking in the corridors triggered a faint memory. A song started playing. It was French class again. Hugo was playing a flute-like instrument. Mr Perez was on the piano. Together the two voices sang in imperfect harmony. The song was happy, the lyrics were not. Everyone else had left, but she wanted to stay, and listen. It would've been great if she knew the song, for she could surely sing. Snapping back to reality, she realized she was in a domed structure which contained a staff room, and a few laboratories. Utility block, they called it. *'I have never seen an SST lab'* she thought, passing a room which contained maps and globes. Then she stopped. Through a slight open door, she saw a harmonium- a familiar friend, and an old, and somewhat frail man. A small cup of tea produced steam next to the mat, on which he sat, both legs folded. It always seemed that artists never noticed others. The man started playing a flute beautifully, in a strangely familiar sound. The music was subtle enough that anyone within approximately five meters radius would hear it. Yet it stopped the girl. She couldn't sing out loud, but she knew what he was playing. A few students clumsily stumbled into the room and came to the man. He stopped, talked to them, and went back to playing the flute. Almost no one was in the area outside the room. There was no one in the room. No chairs were visible. No students glancing at the door of the room. She saw that it was named the 'Music room'. Pleasantly enjoying the feeling of hearing music in school, she noticed the features of the man. His old greying hair and loose clothes made him look wise and venerable. His expression was relaxed, and yet focused. The bell rang, disturbing her and the old man. He stopped playing his flute, and just as soon as the joy had come, it went away. It dissipated into the boring sense of routine. He opened his eyes and looked at the girl sharply. He gestured towards her to indicate that he wanted her to come in. 'What were you doing?' he asked in a gentle voice. 'Nothing Sir," Her feet shuffled. "Just listening, Sir.' She said and smiled nervously. He nodded his head in such a way that it seemed like the conversation was over. 'I'll come back tomorrow,' the girl thought, and walked towards her class.

Two paths

There are two kinds of studying. One of them is fuelled by passion. It doesn't feel like studying, because it is pleasurable. This kind of studying rarely happens. Because the other type is much more prevalent. This other kind of studying includes the act of opening your book, staring at it, and contemplating your horrible life decisions that have led to this moment. French, Science, and English were subjects she used to enjoy the most. Because studying them didn't feel like studying. Because passion, above all, overcame other emotions. These subjects she learnt. Others she studied. Nowadays, even French seemed boring. Lifeless. Purposeless. Discouraged by marks and the lack of confidence had recently amounted to her mugging up answers. Memorizing is easy to do. Was easy to do- once upon a time, when she had had plenty practice.

'But I want to know...'

Research on subjects would often bring unanswerable questions.

'But why do you want to know, Beta? It's not in our syllabus,' most teachers said.

'Oh, my God!' One of her friends had said, 'My brother is in second grade, and he had a book project to do. His teacher cut marks for choosing a book that was 'of a higher level' for the class.'

Then, she dismissed the story. Now, she felt sympathy for the kid. Sure, people in the examiners room had to check thousands of answer sheets, but the work of human beings? A wrong answer is wrong, agreed. But a right answer written in a slightly different way is not wrong. Examiners do not realize that in their hands, they hold the future of children, and they often allow their 'mood' to get in the way. Or at least that's what she was told. The girl then pondered on how the school itself works.

Every day teachers dictate questions and answers. Because it is easy for teachers to check notebooks, if each answer is the same. A question raised in biology class about mutations was recently ridiculed. 'Who told you about mutations? Coaching classes? Beta we are learning about variations, focus on variations.' Different interpretations in an English class are said to be wrong because they aren't the standard ones. French doesn't seem like a language. To her, it seemed like a code now, at least that's the way it was 'taught'. English was no more a subject, it was now a science. A specific science with rules. And Science was a subject in which questions were condemned and explanations were ridiculed.

Daunt O Daunt, Examination, Thy Nature is Such!

It was two days before the science exam. A feeling of loneliness and a sense of foreboding guilt crept into her. It was one of those times when you would just feel that you weren't prepared enough for the exam. When you knew that with some effort, you could do very well, but the amount of courage it took to start wasn't enough. She walked down the road slowly. It was night. A few crickets nearby chirped, blissfully unaware of the sorrow of the tenth graders. The dandia sticks in her hand felt cold. Aimlessly fidgeting around with them, she walked towards a large one-storey structure. Loud and yet nostalgic songs were being sung in imperfect harmony. The classes hadn't started yet, so she went close to a pillar outside the hall, and leaned against it. One foot held upwards, her bottle hung from her hands. Deeply sighing, she stared at the distant view. 'Give me some sunshine. Give me some rain. Give me another chance-I want to grow up once again.' A chorus of middle-aged men and women sang. A distant memory in the girl's brain clicked, and she hummed to the tune. We all love the movie, Three Idiots, but we can't all do what we love all the time, a voice said in her brain. Pondering on the moon above her, she allowed her head to lean back to stare at the trees that covered it.

There were no stars in the sky, but she could see one almost clearly, beaming at her. An imaginary wind blew by, and she felt a drop of water fall on her head. The imaginary star moved in the sky, causing her to believe that she could make a wish. Quickly wishing for good grades in her board exams, she kept staring at the sky. Nearby, a few women came walking by, chatting with each other. Hearing nothing, the girl paid no attention to them, or to the car that drove by or the fact that the teacher had shown up. Everything was silent except for the wind and the rustling of the trees. The water fountain displayed lights, but nothing except for the sound of the water was registered in the dark dreary sub consciousness of the girl.

Her breathing was slow, careful in case it disrupted her thoughts. The different places she had lived in flashed before her eyes, but no jewels liquefied at the centre of them this time. One more place, one more life, she thought. Accepting the same, she wished she could grow up again. The wind caressed her face softly, as if probing her to delve deeper into her thoughts. The sound of the chorus came into her thoughts again – singing the same song, her eyes were open now. Seeing as the other women went inside, she joined them. Once more, the song repeated. 'Give me some sunshine. Give me some rain. Give me another chance-I wanna grow up once again....' The teacher called them to start today's lesson. Outside, she saw the sky, darkened by the purple mass of clouds.

More than you think

A foreigner once came to visit a small, poverty-stricken village in India. There, upon seeing a hut which was adequately broken down to be amusing to him, he then walked towards it. Around him, the few children playing with deflated tires stopped to glance at him, curious at his presence. After sufficiently eyeing him they resumed their frivolous play. A bald plump man in slightly tattered clothes appeared in front of the hut. It was six am, and he was holding a sort of metal pouring container, which evidently held water. Murmuring something, the bald plump man bowed his head and slowly tipped the container to produce a steady stream of water onto the doorstep. The morning sun beamed its light onto the metal and the water producing a magnificently eye-blinding glisten. The observer stopped for the ritual to be completed, then identifying the man as the owner, resumed walking.

He came to the owner and asked 'What were you doing?'

The man now thoroughly aware of the revered looking foreigner said quite simply 'I was pouring water to honour the sun.'

'But this is just water. What can it do?'

To this the man replied, 'It's a little more than just water Sir.'

The man gestured towards his house, trying to invite him. Such little to keep, and yet he wants to share, the foreigner not thought amused. He went in to see a one bedroom house, with little space to sit. However, the humble old man asked him to sit and wait. A few minutes later he came with a small bowl of yellow looking rice with peanuts in it. On the side, he received a ladoo.

'This is all we have to offer, sir.'

'What is this?' the man asked of the yellow rice.

'It is Poha, sir'

'What does it contain?'

'It has chawal, curry patta, aloo, dhania, peanuts and lime juice.'

Recognizing the words for rice, and lime, he asked,

'Is this just lime rice?' 'It is a bit more than that,' said the bald plump man.

Next the man asked about the round edible ball. After listing the ingredients again, the man asked, 'So this is just flour, sugar and butter?'

'It is more than just that, sir,' said the bald plump man again.

By now the foreigner was annoyed at this answer. But he ate quickly, and as the man escorted him out, he saw a woman, presumably the bald plump man's wife, sitting and talking to her child.

'Is that your wife?' asked the foreigner.

'No sir, she is more than my wife.'

Giving up, he then commented on his poor little hut. It seemed he was being taken a little less seriously, unlike a white man in British India should be.

'So, this your hut?' he asked with a smirk.

'It's not a hut sir. It is more than that.'

Clearly annoyed at this repeated remark, the foreigner finally said, 'What is this 'more than' you talk about? Everything is just what it is. It cannot be 'more".

To this the humble man said, 'Sir, the 'more' is what makes us Indian'. 'It is," he hesitated slightly,' more than you can understand' the bald plump man said with a sense of pride. The foreigner stumbled, turned and left, pondering on his words deeply.

Failure

The bitter-sweet thing about life is that most of the people are average. There's always someone better than us – stronger, smarter and we envy them. Failure isn't a friend to most of us, because if it appears too much, we start detesting it. It's a lonely entity, wandering around, latching on to people who will be good to it.

Once in a while it flails across rooms, attaching itself to someone. Perhaps this someone is someone who is trying to rid themselves of it forever, or someone who has forgotten its company and is practically begging for it.

The thing about mediocrity which is most scary, is that it is everywhere. We do not aspire for it. Nobody wants it. When a child is asked what they want to be, they always hope to become someone great, an astronaut, a scientist. And then soon, through the course of years of schooling, after experiencing life, they just fall into mediocrity. Through no fault of their own. A child in twelfth standard often just wants a relatively good college and a stable future. Great is not stable. Good is not great. But by trying to constantly be great, is there something they ignore?

Many of us grow up believing we are special, different, born to do great things. But honestly speaking, the majority of the population aren't. And the constant competition we put ourselves through, to prove to ourselves in fact, that we are better, is crushing.

A teacher once told me to fear the life we'd lead if we didn't get through the entrance test. A life of red buses, bags hanging down on our worn-down shoulders, trying to make ends meet as a middle-class employee, tiffin in our hands. A nine to five job we detest. Reality is, many of those who even get through competition will be leading the same life. And honestly speaking, that life is terrible. The common people- the majority of the people- they aren't geniuses. They aren't riddled with the intention to do anything particularly amazing for society. Some don't want to. Perhaps they can't. Because their focus is on survival.

Thinking about the kind of society we've developed around the world for the majority of us is very disturbing. We've created systems that punish those who aren't "The One Percent". And for what reason? Why is there such a huge disparity between the majority- the general average being and people who have, by luck or inheritance or even their genius amassed great amounts of wealth and a high living standard? Forget about countries, as a planet in general, shouldn't we make life easier for all beings that inhabit Earth? The socioeconomic system is just truly man made, and it's surprising to think that if we didn't want to, we wouldn't have made it up. We tend to blame all this on laws and rules and higher "authorities", but what we don't realise is that in essence, we, humans, we make the rules. So why can't we change them? We made it all up. We can bring it all down. Maybe we could if we didn't have biases against our own. Our own planet inhabitants I mean, not just us.

Blank Paper

A blank piece of paper is the single most frightening thing to an author or an artist. It stares at you, mocking your ability. Questioning you, and your plans. It takes time to overcome the constant fear of whether what you produce will be worth the time and effort. Those who learn to go past this 'activation energy' are what we call 'artists or authors.' And yet even to some of them it is hard to do so. A blank paper deduces all the fear, the tension, and apprehension in a concise, easy to understand manner. For many of us, it is where we lose our minds. For many of us it is a bittersweet memory of what we cannot do. The process works like an enzyme, or a chemical reaction because the work we produce wouldn't exist if we didn't overcome that barrier of energy. The most excruciatingly painful moments of life are the simplest ones. Those thirty seconds or a minute – if we do not persist, we do not produce.

The Star

The star boomed. They say in space voices can't travel. Sound needs a medium to travel, and space is without medium. But now, as the asteroid trembled with fear, it could almost hear the star.

Menacingly, its gaze pierced the asteroid's heart. Then suddenly, its eyes glowed less, and an eerie calm washed over the atmosphere- if you could call it that.

"The year," The star stated.

"They call it the two thousand and twenty," The asteroid answered.

The inner core of the star rumbled with anger, but the voice was still calm.

"What have they done?" The old voice asked. It knew the answer, but it was leading up to something. The asteroid started weeping.

"The little spores- they grew. Into four legged ones. And now the four-legged ones. They-" the asteroid choked.

"You know," the star said. The asteroid nodded, shivering slightly. The usual warmth of the star has started to recede.

"I saw it be birthed," the star said. It glowed slowly. "I-"

"What shall we give them?" The star's inner anger subsided. It grew upset.

"The four legged ones. They feel. They have others they feel for. Others they feel against-"

"Feel against?" The star laughed and then choked. "They have lives-" The asteroid said, crying softly.

"If I were one for embrace, I would indulge- but you know if I did-" the star started to cry as well.

"We gave them their lives. They feel for their own because we gave it to them. We gave it to Earth and then they-"

"I feel sorry-" The asteroid said. The moral dilemma it felt grew. His insides felt twisted if rocks could feel twisted.

"Look at what they've done-"

"The children-"

"And you wish I hadn't given them the spores of the malady,"
The star turned away. Somewhere it felt hurt too, but more so
for its friend. You see, the star could not feel much, but when it
felt, it felt deeply. The star had suffered enough guilt.

"Is there any other way?"

"Do you think they will change?" The star asked. It coughed
violently. The cough shook the galaxy.

"There are many galaxies in which the four legged don't hurt,"
the asteroid said softly.

"Many more in which the four legged never came, ones that
still live." The star looked at the asteroid. Its light dimmed even
further.

"When you said you felt sorry, who did you feel sorry for?"

The asteroid stood there silently, afraid to look the star in the
eye.

"Earth is doing what they want. They do not want the four
legged anymore-" The star said.

"They are driven by rage," whatever courage was left within the asteroid had been summoned.

"The four-legged kill themselves anyway," the star said dismissively. The star closed its eyes. They were so powerful they could see beyond galaxies and for years now they had been fixated on Earth. On the humans. It could not bear to see Earth in pain. It had saw them be born, and had thought they would go after it did. Perhaps a few more years and the star would die. If it wanted to, it could take a few galaxies with it- maybe reunite with Earth. But Earth had wanted life to live. Only they didn't realise it was killing them.

"Any more?" The asteroid asked, now feeling guilty. For it too, felt for Earth. It could not do much, but what it could do, it wanted to do well.

"Rage. Harness what you can from me. I will die soon anyway. Give it to the four legged. When they fall, remember me. And hug Earth. From me too," the star wept.

The asteroid nodded. A few more years and it would give the four legged the rage. And perhaps if they survive through it they will learn. If not, the asteroid knew what had to be done. A star's rage was said to be infinite.

The Milk Business

Today was a very special day. Five more houses just yesterday had subscribed to Ali's milk business. It was a small one, started out of necessity but continued out of the need for a break in the past monotony in the man's life, and of course it would help to earn a little extra money. Routine did not sit with him well and he often got bored of sitting in his shop, waiting for a customer. It felt good to wake up early in the morning and be productive.

Over the past few years, the little stall that said, 'Ali's milk stall' had grown to be not bigger in size but in popularity. The man was a genius, he had invented a way to serve customers without being present at the stall at all! He had installed a little button which triggered a series of chain reactions when pressed. A wire was connected to a small ball of aluminium foil that when lowered would press the call button on a phone kept underneath it. The loud ringing would catch the stray cat's attention, and she would roll out a packet of freshest milk. Of course, through a series of trial and error, and practise, it was decided that the cat had to have some milk at the end of the day to herself. Labour charges were high this season, because she seemed to have given birth recently.

'Why have a phone there at all? There are thieves around you know?' The occasional banter would lead to this frequently asked question.

To this he would reply, 'Trusting your customers makes them happy.' 'Well then, why don't you just let them call directly-from the phone?'

'Well, now, you can't trust anybody, can you?' He laughed, shrugging the person off and masking his face, pretending to be busy.

The nerve! Chaudhary Lal walked away. The man didn't know how to talk to his customers, He harumphfed.

The truth was that he had only constructed such a complicated apparatus, to show off his skills. As a mere shopkeeper and a milk vendor, there were only a few times you could consider yourself better than the others.

When Ali was young, he had dreamt of going to the best of institutes for an engineering course. The desire for a degree pained in him, hurting his already hungry stomach even more-to the extent that to indulge in preparing for the entrance exam was a luxury he dreamt of. He lacked the time to prepare for it. He would be working in the fields many hours before he was allowed to study. And, English was hard to understand – but scientific terms in Hindi were even more of a pain in the neck. He had ended up as a shopkeeper, but he knew he had the brain of an engineer.

A Different Definition of Peace.

There is a certain serenity that is described not as the luscious trees, or peaceful nature. This is the feeling one gets when people who don't even know each other respect and value each other. In a country of mere 7 lakh people, it may not be surprising that no traffic lights exist. The roads are not adorned by stress causing red, yellow and green lights, but instead by a sense of unity, and perfect communication. In Bhutan, the people mostly travel by car. However, when they come across each other, there is a magical moment when everyone knows what to do. Guided by just instinct and the look in the eyes of each other, within milliseconds their hands reach the wheel, and in no time, they cross each other. There is no noise of the obnoxious horn, nor the flashing of signals. But an instant inexplicable connection that allows a conversation to be understood by a flash of light is forged. There is no miscommunication, no error. And it is an insult to modern language. What we study for years to perfect, is done in a few seconds. No words, no grammar, nothing. It is surprising that just instinct, years of evolution, can cause something so amazing. Bhutan teaches us that inside all of us there is a force that can connect to everything, and unleashing it would bring us closer to a society of peace, not one in pieces.

Of Souls and Ghosts

It was nine pm at an old Delhi metro station. The night was young, and had decided to invite the breeze over for a sleepover. Soft winds blew, but cold had also come in. The metro shops were almost closed. The only few people waiting for the 10:30 train were a young 16-year-old girl, and a few shady-looking men. A few calls ago, an emergency had compelled the girl to book the 10:30 train for Meerut. Now tense, she fidgeted with her fingers and glanced at her phone every few seconds. Half an hour was left for the train to arrive.

Suddenly the lights went off. She panicked. A few minutes passed, and she could not see, but she could feel a shift in the position of the men. She switched on her phone light. The others did so too. She thought about the emergency at home. For a moment the girl was in the company of her panic, the dark, and the men who came closer. It wasn't assuring that there was no sound coming from the train tunnel. She stood up and walked to the edge of the platform. The men walked towards her, and she felt upset at the fact that the emergency that she had to attend to might not be attended soon enough. Now the men were closer to her, right behind.

Suddenly the lights came back on. A wisp of smoke appeared on the track. A translucent ghostly white figure appeared. It was an old man wanting a hug. The fact that he looked surreal, healthy, and ageless insulted the purpose of his state. The men moved back frightened. The girl smiled as she wept.

The ghost came to the girl, and although she could not feel, she hugged him. The man felt content and happy. There was a loud screeching noise, the train had just arrived. But the girl didn't get in. The emergency's outcome was clear. The old man's last wish had been fulfilled, too.

The Girl Who Was Good At Everything

Avantika was a 16-year-old girl who was struggling. Before the 11th grade, she was absolutely sure of the stream she'd choose- she knew she had passion for biology and chemistry. Physics came with those subjects, but you can't escape everything. And for all she knew, she would do great with these subjects. In fact, Avantika was so sure of her choice, she even filled out the form way before time. It wasn't a difficult choice until she started the year a month ago, her results had come, and although they were good, she had not done well in science, not bad, just not up to her level. Oh, well sometimes luck just isn't on your side, she thought. Another thing was that Avantika also had passion for literature. It was a compulsory subject, so she needn't choose between science and language. But she had scored a 98 in social studies. 'Meh, I don't like humanities.' Little did she know of the trauma of living with the curse of being good at subjects at the opposite end of the academic spectrum. Slowly but surely, her teachers' repetitive lectures, boring approach and the lifeless enthusiasm of having a sadistic attitude toned the girl's confidence down. It was a fact that in India the 11th grade was one of the tough ones. And so, when she barely got 50% in the subjects, she tried to keep her interest alive. She made a habit of learning as much as possible. Learning, not studying. Perhaps it was more of a disadvantage than an advantage at this point. For again and again she reached new lows mentally and academically. She then studied for hours together, only leaving to eat or sleep or have a small break. Finally, she gave herself an ultimatum. If she would not do well in the half yearly, she would switch to humanities. It was a matter of aptitude vs interest. And she knew that colleges do not look at your application twice if you have passion, they look for grades first. They look at the fact that you had a choice and if you chose the right one. It was time for her to use her abilities as a blessing and not a curse. The college of her dreams was unusual for someone in India, because her dreams were unusual and she knew having unusual dreams was only a pain in fact they were the first of their kind. But Avantika was used to following rule books.

Starry Starry Night

The sea of stars,
This hue of blue,
'Tis of no help,
'Tis of no use.

Stars may watch over
The passage of time,
But they avoid gazing now,
For 'tisn't kind.

As if shaken hands with fate,
It's diamonds dimmed,
It's affinity with destiny,
 Compelling it to refrain.

For it fears and trembles,
Before morn's power,
That some dawn soon,
it's secrets may be ours.

This starry starry night,
A blue sight to behold,

may as well be a cry,
to the sun "withhold!"

The twinkling of stars,
The wretched movement of the earth,
 The inevitable lark,
That flies through light blue.

All its worst fears,
In all its trembling glory,
Its grudge with time,
Its furious peculiarity

It cannot see,
For the stars that blind it
That once the sun goes down,
Navy will again be lit.

Astha

Astha had a preconceived notion of what success looked like. She walked down the gulley with her bicycle on her side, one hand on her side and one on her hip, laden with the weight of her backpack. What she dreamt of for herself was someone else's reality. And without realising what she wanted she decided her whole future ahead. But she did not realise that she did not know what she wanted or maybe she was too afraid of what she really wanted because handling change was not her forte. And when she thought of success in her field, she thought of big houses and Nobel prizes but she did realize the biggest fear she had was of being useless in any way. She noticed a couple of boys playing with tires bereft of air, and thought about their perception of success. What was it that made their eyes twinkle with laughter? Did they feel any disadvantage of being unfortunate? Did they realise what opportunities they missed? She walked on quickly, glancing at her watch. She cursed the time and suddenly glanced at a couple of beggars on the street. Again, she thought, she thought 'what is their idea of success?' do they have any bigger dreams except for those involving a house and money' but when she thought hard, she realised that they didn't need those other dreams. What a strange thought. Are some dreams 'necessary?' What kind of dreams does someone need to have? Moving on, she saw a street vendor, with a sign saying 'Ali's Milk Business,' but she didn't think about anything then. She walked to the shop, bought a couple of milk packets like her mother had asked, and thought about her chemistry paper.

Mangoes and Percentages

For many older people, the idea of school is a nostalgic one, bringing sweet memories to the mind and salty tears to the eyes. They often remember only a few things that come to their mind. While talking to their grandchildren, they omit their struggles, the bullies, and the horrible punishments they would get. So when Shri Hari grumpily came from school with his marks for the year, he was extremely annoyed with his grandfather when he spoke of how he 'walked 6 miles a day to reach school'.

In a small village of Cholapur, the Sri Haridas School of Educated Young Boys had just closed down for summer holidays. The headmaster, dubbed Katthor Sahab, following the sadistic and cruel tradition of - as many students would say - ruining their vacations had handed out their result for the year. In Hari's class 25 faces of regret and disappointment soon turned into a steal-mangoes-from-katthor-sahab party.

The students of class 5, including Sri Hari managed to, in half an hour steal 5 mangoes from the headmaster's private garden. On the way, they had sat down to distribute the pieces among themselves according to the magnitude of the work each had done to obtain them. The sling was used by Kishan so he kept one whole to himself. The bully Swaminathan managed to get one for himself too. After the elites, toppers and the bullies who bullied the toppers had taken their share, it was time to distribute the two mangoes among 'Aam Aadmi', as Viswanathan said in a manner that indicated humour. Shri Hari and the other two boys understood the pun a few moments later only to curse Viswa's horrible sense of humour.

After each child had gotten 2/5th of a mango, they happily left for home.

Now Hari sat down to let his grandfather know he had barely gotten 75%, he was forced to listen to the old man who started with 'jab hum is umar……'.

After learning about his grandfather's heroic adventures and his superhuman power of obtaining mangoes with just one shot, Hari started to explain.

'Tata'

'Tell me how many mangoes did you get?' he said laughing'. 'I got 75-'.

'Mangoes? I used to steal 90! Or 80!' 'No, tata, I-'.

'I have built a legacy! Shame Hari ji! You must practice with me!' He coughed.'

'I actually-'.

'Beta, I am old now but stealing mangoes is a legacy-'.

Till then tata's old friend walked over to him. Hari was frustrated.

'Oh hello! Did you know the prices of mangoes nowadays?' he asked his friend. 'I've heard the price has increased by 50%!' Tata said.

'No, Tata! 75%' Hari started in exasperation.

'75%?' this is a bit too much, don't you think?' Tata's friend said, astonished. Hari wanted to cry.

'No, may be 60% but not 75% definitely' tata said. Hari could strangle a cat.

'But 60% is still a lot. Back in those days...' tata's friend started. Hari clenched his teeth, and punched the wall nearby. Being hard of hearing, the two men ignored him and his gasp of pain.

'Tata!' Hari said.

'Yes Hari?' his grandfather replied, 'why are you so red?'

'I got 75% marks only. How do I tell Amma and Appa?' Hari's face fell as he frowned.

'75%? I told you marks do not matter. When you grow old will you tell your grandchildren your marks?' He laughed patting the boy's back. Hari smiled and left to go to play. He knew tata would manage Appa's mood before he comes back.

After Hari left, tata continued talking. 'Thank god it's not 75%' 'Yes, yes! Or we wouldn't see the fruits this year at our house!' 'I wonder how many years are left...'

'Yes, yes,' His friend said dismissively, 'Well, back in those days, remember headmaster ji? He would...'

Chin Chin Mun Mun

'And so, when Chin Chin and Mun Mun opened the door, their mother came in, and the wolf had gone away,' Serang's grandmother said, soothing the little boy into a deep sleep. Serang went to bed, his last thought being about his cousins who were to arrive tomorrow, he yawned.

The next day Serang got up early and excited. He fell out of his bed and gasped in pain. Then forgetting the fall, he ran up to the kitchen. Angay was already in the kitchen, busy preparing sweet smelling butter tea. Serang was immediately drawn to kewa datsi, and picked up a spoon to taste the cheesy delight. Angay picked up the small boy in her frail arms and put him on the kitchen counter.

'Did you brush yet?'

'Have you been up since 3?' Serang asked mesmerized by the feast in front of him. The food was not adorned in fancy vessels, but then again, has fancy crockery ever disguised the smell of heavenly prepared food to a child?

'Yes I'm trying this new recipe- Jalebi- From the main north part of India' 'Oh, Rahul always talks about it at school'

'Yes, well why don't you go and play now?' Angay asked. Serang nodded his head from left to right and sat there, wanting to talk to her.

After a few hours, Serang groaned while eating his asparagus, and dejectedly walked to the bathroom to take a bath after imagining Angay's disappointed face if he told her he hadn't taken a bath yet. His mood was lifted when he realized that only an hour was left for his cousins to come. As he ruffled his wet hair with the sagging wet towel, Serang pinched his nose and frowned in disgust as he imagined slimy toads sliding down the towel. He had always been told his imagination was exhaustive but he never thought so himself.

An hour had passed and his Agay had woken up too. His grandfather wore his best gho and Angay all her dishes in her best crockery. When the cousins arrived Serang rushed to first greet the adults, and then embarrassed Tshering, Pema Azim, Chimi and Azaan. He couldn't wait to play with them.

Angay forced everyone to sit at the table while she laid the table. The children sat down around the feast, clinging in. The adults sat down on the sofas and held their plates in their hands while talking about the boring things like the government and something called demonetization. Azim Pema sat down on a chair near the sofas. She was in that stage of life where she didn't know where to sit, near the children or the adults. She knew about politics but she was also up to date with what Tom and Jerry were upto recently. She uncomfortably shifted in her seat before going to the table, and took out her phone out of her pocket, staring at it. Typical teenager move.

After an hour or so, Serang decided that he wanted to play with them. He was getting bored. He dragged Tshering and Chimi to the room and told him to take out the chess set. 'Urgh' pema said as she walked towards them. Azaan followed.

'I don't want to play chess!' Tshering said.

'Me neither. Also, it's for two people' Chimi said.

'We can make teams!' Serang said in an excited voice.

'ugh, why don't we just talk,' Azim Pema said.

'Talking is boring......unless you tell us a story Azim!' 'Yeah, you're pretty old now, tell us one!'

Pema felt flattered and insulted at the same time. 'Okay Okay,' she sighed. So there were these two kids- Chin Chin and Mun Mun'.

'You mean goat kids,' Chimi said recognizing the story, 'This is Angay's story!'

'Were they? Okay. So the two goat kids' mom had to go shopping one day.' Serang listened intently. This was his favourite story.

'And she said to them, 'Only open the door when I say- Chin Chin Mun Mun kholo dwar, or else the big bad wolf will come and eat you up!"

'It wasn't the wolf! it was the lion!' Chimi interrupted.

'I clearly remember Angay saying wolf,' Tshering started.

'Excuse me what? Their mom didn't leave them. It was their aunt!' Serang said. 'Aunt? They lived with their father!' Chimi said.

'Are you crazy?' Tshering laughed. 'Me? No! you are!' Chimmi said.

'Listen guys, stop! It was their mom who left and it was the wolf who wanted to eat them.' Pema said with authority.

'Azim, I heard the story yesterday night' Serang spoke politely.

I don't care. I'm moving on' Pema sighed. 'So, the children agreed and the mom left. Soon after the wolf came along, and he told them to open the door. They wouldn't open it, so he got mad and left.'

'Can I just say something? I- this is-there were four kids, not two,' Azaan said quietly.

'Okay how would that even work? Two Chins and two Muns?' Tshering said and Chimmi giggled.

'And so, the next day when their mom went again the wolf tried to get in through the glass window. The kids gathered the sticks and frightened the wolf away. But when their mom said the password the wolf heard it! Then the next day he tried saying it and the children could recognize the voice. They didn't open it so the wolf, who was very angry, tried to come down through the chimney. The kids boiled water in the fire place and the wolf got hurt, and off he ran. When their mom heard this she decided to stay. Together they gathered sticks and boiled water and finally beat him up so much that he never came back. The end,' Azim Pema said loudly. Everyone stopped for a minute.

'Okay but actually, they put hot water on him first and then him with the sticks,' Azaan said.

'Enough, this is what I've heard from Angay. I'm right and you're wrong.' Pema said.

'Azim I heard the story yesterday!' Serang shouted.

'No! this isn't the exact story!' I've heard Angay say that it was a lion!' Chimmi screamed.

'And I heard it a few months ago, and Tshering was sleeping then!' Azaan said.

'Was not!' Tshering snapped back.

'And it was only their mom who beat them up at the end.'

'That's enough! I'm going to Angay.!' Pema started getting up from her seat. Just then, Angay came into the room, and gestured for Pema to sit down.

'What's all this noise?' she demanded in a stern voice.

'Angay it was the lion who wanted to eat ChinChin MunMun, right?' Chimmi blurted out. Pema rolled her eyes.

'And there were four right?' Azaan asked. Tshering sighed in frustration. "ChinChin MunMun?' Angay asked.

'Your story?' Pema asked. Tshering bit his lip. Chimmi looked around nervously. Did Angay not remember her own story?

'Angay, last night's story' Serang said.

'Oh! That! As far as I remember there were these two sheep kids-' Angay tried to recall.

'Goat kids!' They all mumbled together.

'Well, I'm not so sure myself- you see, I keep forgetting the story so I have to come up with new details,' Angay chuckled as she laid down a tray of Jalebis for her grandchildren, who looked at each other, stunned.

New Eyes

We can't even have Saturdays off! Avanti thought as she thumped her feet on the stairs. She sighed with exasperation and reminisced about the innocence and beauty of childhood, she wished it hadn't ended. Her eyes were drooping, dark circles decorating them. Her hair was ornate with rogue strands of black wires whose origins were unknown. Her lips were dry and peeling. Her large sweatshirt hid her just enough to make it seem that she had her life together, but she was falling apart inside. She went ahead into the classroom, and sat down. The teacher would be here in a few minutes. This was ridiculous. *Why should we have to kill ourselves over a test?* She understood the gravity of the classes, how they had to slog like pigs these two years to get into a college, but you can't be cooperative all the time. You can't not throw a tantrum around every once a while. You can't not criticize the society once in a while. It's healthy, isn't it?

Sometimes you just need to let it go. Sometimes it's okay to hate coaching, and not want to do physics, even if it's fascinating. In all honesty though, criticizing the system is a way to distract yourself from the frustration that is life. Avanti was around 5 foot something, 16 years old who bore the weight of the world on her shoulders. Like all of those who were around her, she only wanted certainty in life.

Surety. Just a reassurance that she'll get into her dream college. Just a glimpse of her future. But she had understood recently that as soon as you understand life, the game changes. And right, now this physics class could help her tick the correct option in the NEET paper and could make or break her. And so, when the teacher came in, she opened her notebook and listened intently, a voice in the back of her head telling her to give it her best.

Alia, a classmate, walked in, and hmphfed her way to the back of the class to her seat, annoyed at how perfect Avantika's life was. Perfect grades, perfect life. Even her sweatshirt was so beautiful.

Change

2018 A new era for the LGBT community. Section 377 was about to be struck down by the Supreme Court of India.

People often criticize India for its 'backward thinking'. Not just people who haven't even lived here, but people who have stayed here all their lives. Anshu thought hard about the current affairs of the country. He didn't know what it was – the constant need for something to complain about, or the inferiority complex drilled in to adults that made them say, 'nothing will ever change'.

He reminded himself these were the same people who forget history and tell themselves that the Indian culture is backward. Anyway, he had to get to school and give his exam. His bicycle came to a screeching halt as a group of cows walked in the middle of a road. He cursed in his head and absent-mindedly said 'sorry' out loud. He checked his watch. Twenty minutes were left. He was running late. 'Move aside venerable chaos creators!', he whispered to himself. After a few minutes, he hit the pedal and moved towards the school. When he reached, he locked his bicycle and took out his history notebook to revise. A light breeze brought a flying piece of newspaper to his feet.

He closed the book and picked up the newspaper. A bold headline announced that Section 377 had been struck down.

Anshu smiled to himself.

'Just whims and fancies of the Government. Nothing is actually going to change, boy. Go give your exams,' a teacher touched his shoulder. Anshu frowned, but went to his class quietly. After an hour or so of fidgeting, writing, and racking his brains, the teacher stood up to distribute a circular.

'It's a health card, fill it out quick. Submit it tomorrow,' she said in a bored voice. A few kids were whispering amongst themselves, but the teacher rolled her eyes at them. Finishing the question he was on, he decided to take a little break and look at the card.

He skimmed the paper, postponing having to think of the French revolution and how it changed the world.

As he looked through, something caught his eye. His eyebrows knitted themselves as he looked over the 'gender' option. Curiously enough there were four options – M, F, T and Other. Huh? He read it again. Maybe the 'Other' was a typo or part of another question. No. There was a box next to it for a tick mark, just like there was one next to T. Anshu realized what it meant and smiled. He wanted to take this back and show it to that teacher. Times *had* changed...

Manifesting

'What if there was one exam, that tested your skills and ability to learn? It wasn't based on how much you'd mugged up, but it was based on pure logic?' Avanti had thought just a year ago. And now she was about to give a notoriously difficult test for a science college which aimed to do just that. She reminded herself that she had tried her hardest to study for it and she would get in. She prayed for her performance, and walked into the examination hall. She checked her admit card and found a computer. As soon as the bell rang, she began the test, skipping the Maths section. She jumped straight to Biology. All the questions seemed easy. She heaved a sigh of relief. Then she went on to the Chemistry section. Okay a few questions were strange and new, but it was good. Then she went on to the Physics section and tried her best to do all the questions. This section was comparatively bad, but next was Maths. She attempted two questions. She was sure they were right. As she ended the exam, she deselected an answer from the Biology section that she was unsure of. As Avanti walked towards her father, she regretted her decision. She realized her answer was right. She mentally slapped herself. Urgh. Feeling tense, she thought to herself. She wondered if she was good enough for

Science. How disappointing it would be if after all that hard work, because of that one question she wouldn't get in? Her brain was felt overworked. What if she had made the wrong decision? What if she would be a disappointment? Over the next couple of months, she waited for her interview call. Please God! Worrying after the test was new for her. What would the cut-off be? Could she get over it, if she wasn't selected? Would this be the beginning of the end?

And then it came, a call, just a reassurance. She had gotten through. She had done it. The fear had vanished. In months, she sighed in relief for the first time. She had scored very well. And now she had the confidence she needed.

Exhaustive imaginations

'Huh, so this organism's life cycle involves no reductional division...' Avantika said, yawning deeply. She stretched her hands and glanced at the alarm clock on her table. The lamp flickered and she heard the early birds chirping outside her window. It was still dark outside. She looked at her old biology text book and then at the slide on the microscope on her desk reproachfully. A few seconds later, her head didn't feel like defying gravity anymore and the melatonin in her body protested no more. She was whisked off to a yellow place. Yes, it was very yellow, and what was this! There was yellow sand beneath her feet!

'Next up – Phylum Arthapoda!' A tall pale, yellow haired man said, patting her shoulder. He had a grin on his face, a large backpack on his shoulder, and wrinkles around his eyes.

'Excuse me, what?' she said, still dazed. A frazzled looking Arab boy suddenly ran up to her and said pointing towards nothing frantically,'Magcostheta! Magcostheta! Resolve! Resolve!' and ran off towards nothingness.

'Never mind him, he's a periplenata!'

A swarm of cockroaches appeared before her. She stepped back. The old man jumped across.

'Quick! We must face each phylum to reach Mama Hooba!' he shouted. She stepped over them, and they disappeared.

'Last one-Annelida!' He said.

A slide of water and slimy looking earthworm – like slugs sloshed onto a pool of sand, making it wet.

'I am not getting in there!' she shouted.

'Yes, you are! Come with me!' the old man said, holding her hand, pulling her. 'Let us wheee down that slide!' he said with a childish twinkle in his eyes.

'Huh?' She felt nauseous just looking at them. Suddenly, she was propelled onto the slide, and the view changed. She could now see herself going down. But even though she couldn't control her body, she could feel the slime, the disgust.

'Yurgh!' she cried out as some water covered her head.

The man was across the slide. He started to walk away. She felt a sense of panic. She returned to her body. It was night. A large grey house stood in front of her. She went in to the house as the man guided her towards a large, dark woman who hugged her, almost suffocating her. She wore an orange headband which complimented at least – the colour scheme of her overly bright orange dress.

'Food is this way!' she said in a strange accent. The scene shifted. An Italian guy was now in the living room, having a drink with the woman. 'Mamma Hooba,' he hugged her. She hugged back. The blonde guy was sitting in red sofa, eating a pie. Avantika looked down, she was on a computer, apparently trying to hack in to Mama's wifi. 'Wifi?' Mama Hooba shouted and came over. 'C-H-O-N!' she said. Avantika found herself typing 'C2H5OH + HNO3'.

The scene changed one last time. She felt slight discomfort under her left cheek, and annoyance at the fact that her eyes were closed. She opened them. The lamp on her desk flickered. The paper on which was lying on said 'ethanol-yeast-oxygen'. The alarm clock rang and showed her the time. She sat up straight and adjusted her glasses. Thank God. For a minute it looked like the word HOOBA.

An Epiphany

Avantika squeezed her eyes in exhaustion. She was only listening to the Chemistry teacher because she was interested in the topic he was teaching. They were learning about entropy, or the randomness of the particles in the universe. It was a confusing yet interesting topic, and she listened and related the notes to what she had learnt from her personal research. The others talked, but she smiled like an idiot. She loved it when she could take a concept from one subject and apply it to another. In this case, biology, physics and chemistry- all three were related here. In the back of her naïve head, she subconsciously asked one question to herself. A question, a fire unquenchable about this very topic, whose answer seemed impossible and obscure, a cliff that left her hanging for two years now. A paradox, one could say. Every time she asked, she'd get even more confused. Yet, she listened and smiled in the hopes of finding the answer.

It was a simple question. She asked why systems tend to lose heat if heat brings entropy, and entropy is stable. In the words and terms of normal people, it was like asking why we seek knowledge if ignorance is bliss. Or, why in a heat driven process, heat is rejected. Or even why in every organism's body a steady state means not one where all functions are complete, but one where reactions occur.

Because once they stop, organisms die. Why? If we move towards stability, why do we opt for a less stable route?

She knew little, for as the teacher went on, she paid close attention. As he taught, she looked closer, reading between the lines. He said one sentence that blew her mind. He said 'Some heat must be rejected so that the rest can be absorbed and used.'

As she blanked out for a moment. She understood. Or at least she was close. The chatter and confusion in her class grew and she felt a flutter in her chest. She shivered. She knew. The equations on the board about free energy, entropy, heat made sense and resonated a single answer. She thought of the example, a line from her biology textbook that talked of homeostasis. Her jaw was open; as it had been so far an hour, but she hadn't noticed. She was grinning. She was shivering. The truth dawned upon her, and if there ever was such a thing as a soul, it had been satisfied. Her teacher had been noticing her throughout the class. She had thought about the question and asked him repeatedly. His eyes gleamed with childish glint of happiness and radiated all-knowingness. Of course, the answer was clear now. In homeostasis, in biology, meant a condition necessary for survival where the functions of a system weren't complete and the reactions occurred.

She realized they did so because the functions weren't complete. It moved forward; towards a relatively stable condition whose driving force was instability! If we were satisfied of hunger we wouldn't eat anymore! If things are not unstable, they shall not move towards stability. In simpler words stability was instability. Knowledge was ignorance. It was a cycle! A cycle! What goes up around must come back. Stability – instability – stability.

She felt butterflies. An open pit in her stomach. Her brain had been set on fire. She controlled, somehow, the tears her eyes begged to release. Every atom of her existence laughed. It was beautiful. The gorgeous equations on the board. She felt as though the skies had shed their light on to the board in the class. She felt emotional over the written work on the board. She radiated a knowledge others knew not of. A feeling of weightlessness and hyper excitement took over. She felt in sync with the universe. She just had an epiphany.

Balaghat Boy

In the mundane atmosphere of routine, the sky dulled itself, allowing an unrecognizable shade of blue-grey to radiate itself. The coaching classroom was slowly getting filled for its tri-weekly class. Reina groaned as her auto stopped next to the gate. As she walked out, with her biology textbook in her hands, the usual banter about important topics was being exchanged between the students. She looked around her class, and sat on the first seat- where she always sat. The other students settled in, too. Their eyes twinkled with a maturity far beyond their age- hopefully only temporary- for they knew that now, their 16–17-year-old selves were to decide their future. Perhaps they knew, in the back of their minds, how important their studies were- and yet they sometimes lacked that push- that drive that caused hundreds of aspirants to clear the medical entrance exams. The city had spoiled them, showed them a life they forgot they lived only because of their parents. It had taken their beautiful minds and had extracted the focus- the drive required to do anything. As their teacher rightly said, preparing for such competition- especially in India- a country where the population causes its own pressure on young children- was like exile. Peaceful exile that if they did not endure, they would surely repent. Yet they knew, in the back of their minds- what it took, and they also knew that their denial to do whatever was necessary would lead to a life of miserable averageness.

Between the staccato of misery and hope, a pair of shy footsteps approached the class. A knock on the door, and the door was opened. A tall boy stood there, and his eyes shone with innocence. His skinniness would make any grandmother go on a cooking spree.

"And this is Vedant. He's from Balaghat, he's come here to study with us," the teacher smiled, "Go, sit there-" she showed him an empty spot. The boy flailed across the room, awkwardly making noise as he shifted the chairs and decided on a seat. He opened his plain black bag and took out an old second hand biology textbook and a pencil to highlight whatever he thought was important.

"Now now, don't you city children ruin him. Vedant is a determined young boy and his only work in the city is to study to get into a good college and succeed in life," the teacher said as she opened her guide.

"Chapter 3-" she started.

The rest of the class was quiet except for the periodic quizzing the teacher engaged in. Perhaps in the back of the small classroom two boys muttered under their breaths and paid no attention. Perhaps the girl in the front was thinking about that new bag she'd seen online, and perhaps there were only one or two students who took the class seriously even after the gruelling hours of school, but the boy was adamant on learning. He knew not the luxuries of the nearby pizza place, or the mall that urged people to visit it every weekend. He didn't watch Netflix, and he didn't have TV. He had wifi, but only for whatsapp. He lived away from his parents in the village, with the sole purpose of getting somewhere, finding it hard to find the peace he once found there here.

The mindless ways the city children used their time, was sure to poison his mind, but he kept going, having no other option for a better life, unwilling to let his career be dependent on the shoulder of his parents' already burdened, frail arms. Every once in a week he would visit his distant relative who lived in the city, and in every class, he tried his best.

It was tougher, for him, he could not drop a year, and neither could he afford a private college. He didn't hold an NRI passport, nor a caste certificate. Sometimes he would wonder, wouldn't things be better if the exam was based solely on merit? Or even if reservations were made for the economically weak only?

But thinking about the odds only made it worse.

In the end, he persevered, and even though he was close to losing, he won. Call it luck, or hard work, he tried and he succeeded, unlike many in the class. Many who had already decided to lose, unwilling to fight harder, unsure if they could. It was more luck than work, he thought, but the work he put in had powered him through it.

However, in this moment, at this very exact point of time, in his class, he felt fear and anxiety. He was already getting used to city life, and the hardships he had faced seem to fade away, a strange case of Rückkehr Unruhe that he barely understood himself.

The Worrisome Effects of Overworking

The girl had eyes as large as spoons,
They covered more than half her face;
And behind her glasses they stood unafraid
Her eyes, with shimmer, glazed

The pen moved quickly, stopping in between
For next to chemistry a pair of lips arose;
Smiling, innocent with dimples on her cheek
Her eyes gleaming full of hope

And yet a year later, a painful attempt-
To recreate the girl the artist tried
With hurried strokes and a stressful mind,
She could not remake her eyes.

Finally the artist slowly stood up
And slowly the portrait arose
Everything seemed fine and everything seemed fair
But her eyes were much smaller than before.

Seek and Ye Shall Find

Edward Wilson, an American biologist published a hypothesis, called the "Biophilia Hypothesis," which in short is about how human beings have an innate sense to seek life. We're all told that humans are social animals from when we were young, but there is a huge difference between wanting to be with other humans to interact, and wanting to, as an organism, seek any kind of life. It's why uninhabited, barren or abandoned places tend to come off as unnerving- slightly disturbing.

Apart from being a biological instinct to seek signs of life in any form, when it comes to human beings being "social," one could ask why we do it. Why do we feel the need to connect to others? To form bonds. In many animals apart from seeking a mate for reproduction, having deep emotional connections to others of their kind is unusual.

The problem with this is that ultimately it is inevitable to be "hurt" by someone we have connections with. Even if we don't consider families, friends, people we "love" and "cannot live without" as people who could potentially hurt us, at some point, can and may hurt us. Because everyone is different, yes, but logically shouldn't we stop wanting to interact further?

Someone who has emotionally hurt us in some way- that interaction- shouldn't we stop trying to "fix" it? Perhaps if we weren't so emotionally invested in other people and their own thoughts and actions, we wouldn't be hurt if they did or said something we disagree with.

As biological entities, anything that causes harm to us, people who make us upset, we should instinctively avoid. Any sort of harm done to us should kick in an instinct to stay away from that person. After all, we don't put our hands into boiling hot oil after experiencing or even knowing how it'll hurt us. But yet, we seek others. For validation, as if our own conscience doesn't know what we're doing is right or wrong. For some sort of signal that we're okay and we're being normal. Why can't we stop interacting with each other even after disagreements or fights? Why do we approach people who everyone else has warned us about?

Knowing and understanding the other person's predicament, we still manage to irk everyone around us at some point of time.

Because we cannot know everyone and we will do whatever we want ultimately. Isn't it better, then, to construct a bubble around our deepest darkest secrets and personality and opinions to protect us from being hurt by anyone? Especially those who we know can make us feel upset? Why do we want people to stop fighting?

Why do we want our issues to dissolve and for "everything to be fine again"? Why do we feel the need to "make up" with people or talk about issues?

To take it one step further, there are people who allow others to hurt themselves. Many people who stay in an abusive relationship -of any kind don't realise that they are in one. Call it Stockholm Syndrome, the fact remains that human beings often don't know what is good for them. We pride ourselves on being a smarter species, a more intelligent one, but at the end of the day, what we truly seek is a life where apart from satisfying work, the people around us are those who we admire and love and respect. The most human thing we have is not our intellect or our inventions, but the connections we form in day-to-day life.

The Cadaver

Cadaver. The word meant nothing to her. And yet as she walked down the hallways of her own mansion, she wondered if she was one. Outside it was raining heavily. Someone was playing the piano in one of the rooms on the ground floor. The insides of the large house dimmed, as if the lights themselves knew what had happened. They dimmed to show respect. To tell her they knew. And that they would remember, even if no one else would. They told her, as she walked down the spiral stairs that they would be ready for her, if she chose to visit again. Perhaps it was the rain that dimmed them-for they were just flames. But it wasn't. It couldn't be. The lights of the mansion never dimmed in the face of rain. They would grow brighter.

The large velvet curtains seemed black and not their usual maroon. They swayed and shuddered under the compulsion of the wind. The staircase railing was cold to the touch. Perhaps she was not even touching it. But she could not tell. She remembered nights she and her lover would go dancing. The large open ballroom in the middle of the house lay tonight, unlit and dusty. Two women, dancing till their feet cried. Her feet today felt tired. It was almost like she was unable to walk. And yet she almost floated across the staircase, slowly taking it all in. Her mansion. This beautiful place she had built to grow old in.

She could not remember exactly what had happened in the afternoon. Her mind was hazy. She gathered courage to walk to the kitchen. After all, it was a rainy night and she ought to have something warm. Especially for her throat. She was reminded of the things she had yet to study. Immediately a list was made in her mind. She remembered she was working in the middle of the night before, working with the bodies she had gotten from the grave. She remembered exactly where the charcoal and the parchment lay- in her study room on the first floor. The body of the woman in the room had had to be addressed immediately. If they found out about it, it would be terrible. She could be burnt to death for her defiance to let the dead go. Grave-robbing was a crime. She had always considered her aspirations to be worth the isolation and sacrifice. And after all, she had a lover and an abandoned palace to live in till the end of time. It was enough. Someday someone would look to her notes, wouldn't they? They would learn from them, study them. Help people. If not in this life, she felt at least in some other life she would finally be able to study medicine properly. Without comments about her being a woman putting her down.

"Dominion. The world is about dominion," her mother would say to her. Her mother had become cold and bitter when her husband had left her. And yet, it was in the days after the divorce that she made the most sense it seemed.

The kitchen was in shambles. She would have to address this mess at once. But as soon as she thought about cleaning it, she remembered she had to get back to her notes and diagrams. The cadaver she had gotten would rot soon and she would also have to get rid of it. Before dawn, she was determined to draw and note. She realized she would also have to run to the market to get more charcoal.

Sighing, she looked around. A small fireplace burned, but she could not feel its warmth. She cursed herself when she realized she had run out of tea. The tea leaves in the jar looked like dust and smelled quite bad. They must have caught moisture and gone bad. She walked out of the kitchen, and tripped a little. However, she must have picked herself up very quickly because she was right back on her feet. In a puff of frustration, she went and sat in the other piano room. The music still went on in the main piano room, and she smiled, thinking of who must be playing at this hour.

The room she was in- she sat down on one of the chairs, rocking herself. She hummed to the tune she heard and looked around. The carpet looked dull and cold. She was afraid water must have seeped through to there as well, and once again she thought of the bodies she had recently acquired. Of their nature. Of course, their state- which was very much not living- was upsetting. But she doubted people knew much about medicine now. Frankly, her job was an important one. Shunned from society and living off of scraps, she was convinced of the importance of the documentation of the human body. A marvellous creation. Perhaps if they'd have let her practice medicine and study instead of shoving down the frivolous idea of marriage, she would not be drawing her precious diagrams. But now, all that mattered, was preservation of charcoal on parchment, and the constant and careful acquiring and disposing of bodies.

She wondered when they would understand. If she would ever live a comfortable life, being a woman-and also in love with one; having the supposedly eccentric idea of understanding the body before healing it. Healing living beings would have sufficed her passion, but for now, she dealt with the dead.

Although she felt not morose or upset. Yes, days would get melancholic but she was determined. She wondered how others didn't understand how absurd it really was to erratically treat the body without fully understanding it.

But some days she wondered if cadavers could still see. If they knew. If she had housed their spirits. If they were angry with what she was doing. Surely if they were and she knew they were, she would drown in guilt- she wished no harm to those who had succumbed to the light. And yet she wondered whether cadavers felt. And if they were still people, although they were bereft of their beings. Sometimes she felt she looked at them as objects. Objects for her to study and learn from. But that thought was almost immediately stopped as soon as she repeatedly realized her work was important. Today however, in this cold cold room where she sat, trying to warm herself with the fire of the fireplace, she could not help but think.

The carpet and its luxurious design looked back at her as she sank into the chair. She could hear thunder and she saw lightening. The room reeked of death. Some form of guilt came to her and she could not shrug it off. Would the people who had given their lives be okay with how she studied their bodies? Perhaps they watched from afar in contempt and someday the repercussions of all her actions would suddenly overcome her and be her downfall. She felt upset and angry. Her head was hazy and heavy. But she did not feel like sleeping. She turned around in her chair and to her surprise her body was no longer corporeal. She felt light. Her feet- they didn't look like they were touching the ground. She ran to the main piano to see her lover. A body had fallen over and it had hit the piano. It was her. The body was burnt.

Suddenly everything that happened came back to her. She realized the tea leaves weren't bad. They were burnt. The carpet around her had turned to dust. The piano was charred. The curtains had holes in them. There was the smell of smoke that suddenly flooded the room. She remembered the afternoon.

Her breath- she could not feel her breath anymore and she looked around for help. But no one was there to help her. In a fit of utter rage, she ran to her study. She went to the bathroom immediately, and looked at the mirror. She could not see anything.

As she stepped out of the bathroom, she turned the chair where she sat before, afraid of what had happened. They had found out.

And instead of the one cadaver she was studying, she saw two. She looked around and from the wall emerged the figure of a ghost. The cadaver. Realization dawned upon her as she cried. She looked at the face at first in horror. And then her heart sank. A small smile came from the face. And in those eyes she stared into, suddenly she knew. She knew. The question she had been asking had been answered. There had been a fire. But by dumb luck, her notes had been untouched by the flames. The ghost nodded. She nodded back. It was time for the spirit to leave the mansion. And she knew it was time to go back to the piano room to be with her lover. She realized the great truth. That she was a cadaver. A charred body. And she also knew if someone were to study her body, a strange sense of good-doing would help her move on. The ghost withered away, and so did she- to her lover, who had been waiting for her.

They left for the woods, never looking back at the mansion. And they knew in a strange and twisted way that their love, as well as the charcoal and paper was immortal as should be always. In another time they would be remembered. The illustrations would live. She could not wait to give in to the light. Cadaver. Perhaps the word meant something to her after all.

The Sonnet

The back of an old coaching notebook has, somewhere,
written in it, a sonnet. I wrote it one day in class, waiting for
the teacher to come. It was about loneliness, and how I felt
out of place as I often do. There were moments- time between
classes, perhaps a few lunches, where maybe the absence of
one person was one too many. I felt the need, before, to add it
to this collection of stories and memoirs. I was very proud of
coming up with it. Sonnets are hard to write, you have to keep
track of the syllables and the number of words. The bridge, the
number of lines. That is, if you are to write one in lieu with the
general idea of a sonnet. That day, as I sat there, pretending to
not care that I had no-one to talk to, it just came to me. I do
remember the first line- it went like "Why do I wallow in such
misery?". The rest of it, however, I do not remember anymore.
I'd like to read it again, because I remember being very proud
of coming up with it.

I have observed that I write when I am overwhelmed with
emotion. I used to keep a diary of sorts in which I would pen
down my thoughts and now while looking at them it suddenly
hits me that I would only write when I was either extremely
upset or extremely happy. It seems to me the ordinary was

never special for me- nothing worth remembering, nothing worth noting down. And to a certain extent, I regret having not written about the days I would just get up, have a nice breakfast, go to school, and talk to people. Learn about things, enjoy the lunch break, play with a few of my friends, come back home, and enjoy a packet of onion pakodas while watching CID.

I do remember those days. I do. I remember the parties we threw for guests. The amazing food my mother would cook. The pretty mocktails and the salt-lined crystal glasses for the Virgin Mary drinks. The bottles of cold drink me and my brother would greedily eye before the guests had come- at which point they would mysteriously disappear. We would dress up nicely, and go inside a room, not wanting to really interact with the guests unless children of our age were to come. We would be allowed, for those days particularly, to occupy ourselves with whatever we wanted to watch on the big screen, stopping occasionally to refill our plates with mini sandwiches during the appetizer rounds. By dinner time, it would get late and we'd have already filled our stomachs with the chips and the sandwiches and other such delectable goodies. We'd have had a good share of the cold drinks as well. We'd fall asleep, only to be woken up after the guests left, made to change, and quickly get into bed.

I remember the days we'd very occasionally go to play tennis or swim in the swimming pool where my mother would take a box of Threptin biscuits because she knew we'd get hungry. I remember the vacations we took, to the Lakshwadeep islands and Andaman and Nicobar. I remember going to Disneyworld in the US. I remember the Kala Ghoda Festival, where me, my brother, and my best friend would go with our mothers to enjoy full days. Treks and trips and hotel stays. All of these things I've done with my family. Every second, enjoying it- not knowing they'd be such fond memories. My childhood was filled with an explosive amount of worldly experience, at a very young age I learnt to adapt to different cultures, and to appreciate the world's many differences. At every stage, in every place, I made friends and am still making friends. When I look back at the people who I've met, the places they are from, it's crazy to think about all the different lives I've led. Maybe I do not have extremely close friends, and perhaps I never formed decades old friendships like people who live in one place their whole lives do. But I do remember, and I do know, that at every step, I had- and have- a family that cares for me and is always my constant.

Now that I note down every "normal" event in my life, I realise that every second of it is extraordinary. None of it is or ever was normal, and I don't think anyone's life, for that matter, is just normal. It's the little things more than the big ones that we must look for. To romanticise every aspect of the current. To note and observe. While I live in Mangalore, I try to note the little things happening all around me. All around me, people fall in love, blue love birds drop feathers right before my exams- as if on cue, and perfect flowers fall. All around me I see cats roaming around, a specific koyal (I think) that loves to fly around the hostel. The way the light falls on the basketball court when it's early morning. The smell of the rain, and the smell of freshly cut grass when they cut the grass. The smell of formalin in the dissection hall and how sometimes it stings- and other times it feels like a subtle welcome back to college. The way the Haematology lab always has this blue stain in little bottles kept around the corner. The way that each person's logbook was made to be exactly identical and yet when we are to remove ours from a pile of logbooks, we know exactly which logbook belongs to who.

Maybe the diaries I wrote should have had more of these little things. But I do not regret it anymore, because while writing right now, I realise I do and will remember all of these things. And even if not, to know they brought me joy once is enough. I was never alone, and I never will be alone. The only reason for the feeling of loneliness I felt was because I thought loneliness is comforted by just other people. And that, I now know and realise, is far far away from the truth. I do not know where the notebook is- or what page I've written that sonnet in. I still do want to read it; I was very proud of it. But I don't think I will relate to it anymore. And I thank the universe for that.

The Secrets of The Uni(multi)verse

A multiverse theory is very fun to think of. Since it can't be disproved, it might even be possible. In my mind, when I think of alternate realities and universes, I think of different versions of myself doing different things. Different decisions I might have made, different career choices, different friends I must have made, or am making. A part of me has always wondered whether multiple Vaibhavis exist simultaneously and it brings me joy to think about it. Because in a reality, I own a little bookshop by the countryside. I wake up and make myself coffee in my beautiful cottage and I stroll around my garden and admire the flowers and plants. In a reality, I took maths and I'm studying quantum physics and discovering the secrets of the universe. In an alternate reality, I must've taken humanities, and must be working to become an IFS officer. In a reality, I've taken English as my major subject and have published multiple books. I have a beautiful large wooden house and each evening I sit by the fireplace and read myself to sleep, only to wake by the smell of dewy morning air. I write, and I study, I teach and I learn. And I am content. Somewhere far away, I've taken up pure science and fuelled my passion for biology. Somewhere somehow I've discovered the cure for cancer. I work in my own private lab and conduct research that will help generations to come. I work for an organisation that helps fund the research. I have a never-ending list of research ideas and I keep conducting them to my heart's content. In a reality, I make art and sell it. Sculptures, paintings, and other little things. I spend my time joyfully moulding clay into figures. In another reality I'm preparing to go to outer space. I spend all my time training for how to live there, and am constantly excited by the possibility of an outer-space experience.

In different realities, I do different things. Perhaps a Vaibhavi somewhere did get into AIIMS. Perhaps a Vaibhavi is writing another book. Perhaps a Vaibhavi is pursuing her love for music.

The comforting thing about this is that it may be true. I may actually be doing different things in different realities. In different universes. And sometimes I look at the sky and wonder, if other Vaibhavis think the same. If they too, wonder if a Vaibhavi somewhere took up medicine. If a Vaibhavi is studying biology, if a Vaibhavi took arts or if a Vaibhavi took maths.

I truly feel satisfied, feeling accomplished and fulfilled, having done and also simultaneously doing all the things I could ever do and being all the things I could ever become. In a way, I feel I've done them all. That all the choices I've made, or haven't made, have still somehow come into my life in different ways. In my own different lives. Somewhere, a me is thinking the same thing right now. And in this wonder and appreciation for the vast space we live in, the pointlessness of everything we do on Earth doesn't feel pointless anymore.

www.ingramcontent.com/pod-product-compliance
Lightning Source LLC
Chambersburg PA
CBHW060943120626
46557CB00003B/1113